Usborne
Forgotten Fairy Tales

The
Sleeping
Prince

Retold by Andy Prentice

Illustrated by Maria Surducan

Reading consultant: Alison Kelly

About
Forgotten Fairy Tales

People have been telling each other fairy tales for thousands of years. Then, a few hundred years ago, collectors began writing the stories down. The ones that became famous were the ones that reflected the ideas of the time.

These stories had patient, polite princesses such as *Snow White* and *Sleeping Beauty*. The tales with bold girls fighting their own battles were ignored.

This series brings to life the stories of those forgotten brave and brilliant girls…

Contents

Chapter 1

A skipping rhyme

Long, long ago, there lived
a princess who was very,
very bored.

She was never allowed to go fishing for sharks, or to climb tall trees. She couldn't even get her dress crumpled.

Instead, she had to watch everyone else having fun.

The princess imagined going on thrilling adventures to faraway places. She became an excellent storyteller.

One day, she was imagining fighting pirates, when she heard a sweet song.

In the courtyard below,
children were skipping
and singing:

The prince he sleeps and does not wake...

...until midsummer's evening.

The princess was
curious. She'd never heard
the song before.

"My mother sings it to me. She says it's a true story," a girl said. "Every year, a sleeping prince wakes for just one hour, on the evening of San Juan."

9

"He will sleep forever,"
the girl added. "Unless he
wakes up and sees a princess
at his bedside."

"I'm a princess," thought the
princess. "I could save him."

"The song says to find the castle, the princess has to break some iron boots." The girl shrugged. "That part sounds crazy to me."

The princess wasn't worried by these strange directions. At once, she started to plan...

Chapter 2

The House of the Sun

The princess asked the royal cobbler to make her a pair of iron boots. "Please deliver them in secret," she said. "They're a surprise."

A few days later, she clumped
out of the castle and clanked
towards the setting sun.

The princess was wearing
three pairs of socks, but her
new boots rubbed painfully.
Before long, her feet were
covered in blisters.

13

Still, the princess clumped and clanked on until the morning. At last, she came to some magic woods.

In the woods, the princess met a friendly old lady. "Do you know the castle of the sleeping prince?" she asked.

The old lady had never
heard of it.

My son, the Sun
might know.

"But I'm afraid he will hurt
you!" said the old lady. "He's
very bright but oh, he is so
grumpy sometimes."

The princess was not afraid.
She went back to the old lady's
house and hid in a wardrobe.
That evening, the Sun burst in.

"I smell human flesh!"
blazed the Sun. "I want to
eat it!"

"Simmer down, you silly
boy," said the old lady.

"Have you heard of the castle of the sleeping prince?"

Do you know where it is?

"I've never heard of him or his castle!" roared the Sun. "Maybe my sisters, the stars, will have an idea."

Snuggled in the wardrobe,
the exhausted princess fell
asleep. The old woman woke
her at dawn.

Over breakfast, the princess
talked to the star sisters. They
had come back from their
night's work in the sky.

None of the sleepy stars had heard of the sleeping prince.

"But maybe the Wind will know," chimed the smallest star. "He goes everywhere and is always on the move."

Chapter 3

The House of
the Wind

So the princess set off in her
iron boots and clumped on –
clanking with every step – for
a long time. Her feet were
bleeding, but she grimly
ignored her blisters.

In the late afternoon, she met another old lady in the woods.

I'm looking for the castle of the sleeping prince.

Never heard of it!

"My son, the Wind, might know," said the old lady. "But I'm afraid he will blow you away. He's very grumpy and oh, he is so loud."

The princess wasn't afraid.
She went to the old lady's
house, and hid in her wardrobe.

Soon the Wind burst in.
"I smell human flesh!" he
roared. "I want to eat it."

"Pipe down, you silly boy," said the old lady. "Do you know the castle of the sleeping prince?"

"Hah! That's easy," hooted the Wind. "If you leave this house by the back door, you'll find his castle."

When the Wind had gone, the princess clanked through the back door. Outside, a towering thicket of thorns blocked her path.

The princess fought her way through, clomping a path with her iron boots. Soon, the boots crumbled away completely.

Instantly, a magnificent
castle appeared before her. Its
huge doors stood open.
The princess went in.

Chapter 4

The sleeping prince

The castle was richly furnished but almost empty. A solemn maid took the princess to the prince's bedroom.

The prince was lying in a
large and comfortable bed.
He looked young — about the
princess's own age. He was
also fast asleep.

The princess sat down at his
bedside to wait.

Outside, she heard fishermen's shouts, and seagulls screeching over the cliffs.

Inside, dim light crept through the curtains. The princess listened to the slow ticks of the clock and the prince's soft breathing.

The princess was trapped inside a castle once again. So, once again, she began to tell a story...

It was a grand adventure.

Time passed quickly. Every
evening, the maid brought her
food and water.

Every morning, the princess
took up her story. Days passed
and the prince slept on.

Meanwhile, the story grew
longer and longer. The princess
wove the prince into
her story.

Together, they climbed
volcanoes and dived deep into
sunken cities. Together, they
crossed storm-tossed seas and
dusty deserts.

Together, they fought off
giant monsters, masked
bandits and ferocious beasts.

Weeks and months slipped by. Seasons came and went.

The princess barely left the prince's bedside. She always watched the prince's face. She hoped that he was listening.

Each twitch of his lips and every small smile was a clue. Slowly, slowly, a strange thing was happening.

Little by little, the princess was getting to know the prince.

She knew he was brave. She knew he liked dogs, moonlight swimming and peanut butter sandwiches.

And slowly, slowly, little by little, the princess grew to love the prince.

Chapter 5

The festival of San Juan

One day, the princess heard faint music and fireworks. The village below the castle was celebrating midsummer.

36

The princess was distracted by her story. She had no idea San Juan's day had finally arrived.

The princess loved music very much. She went onto the prince's balcony.

At that very moment, the prince opened his eyes. The first person he saw was the maid. He thought she was the storyteller of his dreams.

The maid took her chance.

The prince had been asleep
for many years. He was still a
little groggy. "Here's a pretty
puzzle," he muttered.

He looked from one
girl to the other.

"I know!" He smiled.
"Answer me this: what
was the name of the old
hermit crab at the bottom
of the sea?"

40

"I don't know," said the maid.
"What a peculiar question."

His name was
Canute!

"I loved that bit of your
story," said the prince.
"He was a very silly crab."
"You heard it all?" asked
the princess.

"I dreamed every word." The prince took her hand. "Thank you for breaking the curse — but thank you even more for your story."

They were both far too happy to be angry with the maid.

Chapter 6

A royal wedding

Wedding Invitation
You are cordially invited to join us
to celebrate our wedding at Cliff Castle
on July 7th at 3pm.

The princess and prince
sent out invitations to their
wedding the next day.

The princess's parents had
been worried sick. They were
delighted to hear that she
was safe.

The whole kingdom was invited, along with the Sun and the Stars and the Wind (and their mothers).

The castle had been silent for so long. Now it was filled with music and laughter and the rich smell of the feast.

The princess and the prince ruled the kingdom together for many happy years. They never stopped loving each other...

...because the prince had imagined her in his dreams, and the princess had dreamed of him while she was awake.

About the story

This fairy tale is based on an old Spanish story 'El rey durmiente en su lecho' which means 'The king sleeping in his bed'. There are other versions in French and Arabic.

Designed by Sam Whibley
Series designer: Russell Punter
Series editor: Lesley Sims

This edition first published in 2020 by Usborne Publishing Ltd.,
Usborne House, 83-85 Saffron Hill, London EC1N 8RT, England.
usborne.com

48

In our retelling, the
princess has become a
storyteller of magical
tales herself.